Voices

in the

Waterfall

© 2008 Beth Cuthand

Library and Archives Canada Cataloguing in Publication

Cuthand, Beth, 1949-
Voices in the waterfall / by Beth Cuthand. -- New rev. ed.

Poems.
ISBN 978-1-894778-58-9

I. Title.

PS8555.U846V65 2008   C811'.54   C2008-903824-X

Printed in Canada

Printed on Ancient Forest Friendly 100% post consumer fibre paper.

www.theytus.com

In Canada: Theytus Books, Green Mountain Rd., Lot 45, RR#2, Site 50, Comp. 8
Penticton, BC, V2A 6J7, Tel: 250-493-7181
In the USA: Theytus Books, P.O. Box 2890, Oroville, Washington, 98844

Patrimoine canadien   Canadian Heritage

Canada Council for the Arts   Conseil des Arts du Canada

BRITISH COLUMBIA ARTS COUNCIL
Supported by the Province of British Columbia

On Behalf of Theytus Books, we acknowledge the financial support of the Government of Canada through the Book Publishing Industry Development Program (BPIDP) for our publishing activities. We acknowledge the support of the Canada Council for the Arts which last year invested $20.1 million in writing and publishing throughout Canada. Nous remercions de son soutien le Conseil des Arts du Canada, qui a investi 20,1 millions de dollars l'an dernier dans les lettres et l'édition à travers le Canada. We acknowledge the support of the Province of British Columbia through the British Columbia Arts Council.

Recycled
Supporting responsible use of forest resources
www.fsc.org Cert no. SGS-COC-003153
© 1996 Forest Stewardship Council

FSC

Acknowledgements

My sincere thanks to the good folks at Theytus Books who keep me published in spite of myself. Thank-you Anita Large for your patience and great sense of humor; Louise Halfe for your editing prowess and clear headed direction. Thanks Jeannette for continuing to remember that the stories are larger than ourselves.

And as ever, I thank my mom and dad, Chris and Stan Cuthand, for supporting me through the lean years and the years of plenty. For my brave sons Steven, Luke and my husband Gerry who inspire me to wrestle those words down on paper: thank-you, thank you, thank you.

So I may fly
so I may walk
so I may love
so I may give voice

to a new song for a new time.

I give you back.

Voices

in the

Waterfall

_____

by Beth Cuthand

New Revised Edition

THEYTUS BOOKS

Voices in the Waterfall

By Beth Cuthand

Our Sacred Spaces

Invasion

Revolution

Return to Our Sacred Spaces

Our Sacred Spaces

Songlines at Dreamer's Rock
for Luke

You know me by my dress   green mallard blue
      swaying deep in   this cave of bones
      Indigo dreamer   dance with me.

You hear my purple light   singing to dawn and dusk
  and you know it too: beginning and endings are
  all one fearsome love   for the gifts of dreamers and
fools.

I know you by your   clear blue songs
  and boy's breath
  dreaming life   in the Indigo night.

I hear your star time singing   and I know it too:

    Time and stars end
      where God lives.

Purple hearted dreamer   sing with me

To this ancient earth   these song lines at dreamer's rock

    Life is.
    Life is.

I am the Voice

for Morningstar

I am the voice of waves crashing on raw stone shores.
I am the voice of raindrops on glass refracting rainbows.
I am the voice of night whispers, moans and soft sounds
of skin on skin, bones reverberating wild delight.

I am the voice of fierce some bear woman doing battle
for lost souls seeking light.

I am the voice of thunder rumbling deep fire over
earth tears bringing flight.

I am the voice of mother cooing love songs to newborn.

I am the voice of woman calling wolves, cracking ice shields
covering broken hearts.

I am the voice of earth, sky, wind, fire.
I am womb, breasts, hips.

All of this.

She brings the Dreams

...wades through sky
feathered breath touching
the heart of all.

Buffalo keep the sun
returning
to the sea grass.

Life continues
season to season
birth to death
to birth to death.

She sings the songs
spins the world
that bring the winds
stirs the dust
of blue horses

humming

clouds whisper
sweet rain and horses
dancing in prairied night.

Stones speak
to little people who
have known
her.

This is the secret
they whisper:

There is no magic here.

She smiles at us!
Weeps for all our delusions
brings dreams to fill
our emptiness.

She brings the dreams.

She saves the sight

the sound of light

in the night.

Horse Dance
To Emerald Mountain

l

I am
an ancient grey stone
burned to ash
in the heat of the sweat.

I am
a prayer
a song
a raw green stone;
dusty unpolished
piece of the earth.
I am as clean
as complete
as I am.

My journey begins.

ll

galloping, galloping, galloping, galloping
across a clean brown plain
toward the blue mountains
stretching, stretching, stretching
into infinity.

The horse
the horse
the horse and I
are one.

galloping galloping

across the brownness
the dark mountains
loom

danger   danger

We run

What is this I see?
What is this?
An Emerald Mountain;
green upon green upon green

heart beats
drum beats
hooves beat
drum beats earth beats
heart beats
heart beats
in time   in time
toward the Emerald Mountain

safety
peace

Do I fear the truth?

The sun shines
without consent
upon the clean brown plain
the dark mountain
the horse
and I:
eagle child
horse dancer
bear stone woman
child of peace

who am I
who am I

Fear

The sun is setting
green darkens to black
black upon black
a silhouette
in the eastern sky.

Do rainbows shine at night?

lll

The sea
existed
at the beginning,
like the water
of the womb
crashing
thundering
making for the Maker
the beginnings
of Life.

Mother Earth smiled
Father Sky rained
and Earth waited,
pregnant, powerful
under the waters
for Creation's birth.
I was there
at my birth
hearing the sea
thundering

on the shores
of the womb.

The Sky-thunder,
Life-giver
roared
and Mother Earth
brought me forth
groaning
moaning
pushing me
from her womb

and I
bloody
crying out
for Life.

IV

galloping galloping galloping galloping
across the clean brown plain
I search for my Emerald Mountain
black upon black now
cold
in the midst of death.

galloping galloping
the horse and I
dance
and
dance
in the cool light of the night.

Gone

from the warmth of the womb

Gone

from the tit of the Earth

I am alone

The horse has gone

My friend

My friend
Why do you leave me now?

In the darkness of the night
I rest
bereaved
I see black
lighten,
colour,
leave for a new day.
The morning voices say:
Enjoy this freedom now.
Feel the wind and sun.

The horse leaves you to remember.
Be aware of your comprehension
of matters made in
another land.

I remember my Grannie Bess
at the moment of her death.
Three thousand miles away
I lay supine,
gasping for breath
dying

as my namesake.

Hers
the physical death,
a merciful death
of the seed
of the seed
of me.

My death
a different death
of a way of life
become irrelevant.

My name died with her
I am
a nameless one
Journeying to find

V

The horse returns
head tossing
hooves prancing
impatient for the dance

We face east
catching the light of the sun
glinting
gleaming
glowing
on the face
of the Emerald Mountain
I shiver
the horse rears
leaping forward toward

our fate.

galloping galloping galloping galloping
the dark blue mountains
rise before us now
steep
treacherous
testing the dance.

The sun shines
unmercifully hot.
The Eagle screams.

My heart beats
the sound as loud
as the waves
thundering
on the edge of my womb.

The Emerald Mountain calls:
Leave the horse,
walk alone,
climb my shimmering face.

I am alone
unnamed and afraid

Do I walk on?

The horse waits
I remember the warm brownness
and the breast of my mother
safe but always
becoming   becoming
galloping   galloping
across the warm brown plain
never here

but always coming here.

My heart speaks
telling me
the nameless one
to walk on
to climb the steep face
of the Emerald Mountain
green upon green
upon green
its heart hidden
in dark rumbling mist
fearsome thunder.

VI

The Eagle screams
screams
I must walk on

what lies at the summit
of my Emerald Mountain?

What truth is concealed
in the rumbling mist?

I am numb with fear and hunger
chilled, thirsty
tired and afraid

There is no comfort
no safety
no promises
in this path
I choose to walk.

As if of its own volition
my spirit reaches out
a salient river
sinuous, fluid
touching green upon green
I hear the Eagle screech.

I feel the rumbling, coursing blood
of the mountain
I see the mist rise
and there upon the summit
I see me
dressed in wings

I am
dancing   dancing
surrounded by the ancient ones
and the hooves of horses
beating sounds of the mountain
in time with my wings
smooth emerald
carved by crystal light.

Vll

I am clear green stone
gleaming polished
piece of the Earth

I am a clear blue pool
washed by a waterfall
dusted in mist

I am the Emerald Mountain
selfless
unfettered free.

Notawayohtayohkhan wants Stones

for Sharlene

Notawayohtayohkhan wants stones.
The coyotes run with night.
They call me and I shiver.
In the dark, the spirits come.
            I sing and play with them.

When people die they travel
and we sing them to the other side.
They eat with us before they go.
People cry then laugh.
That's the way it's done.

At night I dream.
I visit her. She is very very old.

She *is* the stones I find.

Someday I will be a woman
with wrinkles
then
I will run with the coyotes at night.

Earth/Sky Trilogy

He

to Little Johnny and Funny Bear

He is the father of the earth
stained brown by sun and wind,
wandering far in search of sunrise.

He is the son of sun and brother of moon
ripe as a tree laden with fruit,
giving sustenance to cloud walkers.

He is a warrior prince, hunter of buffalo,
gardener of corn, keeper of sacred dances,
drums, rattles and funny faces

He is the grandfather dressed in cedar
gathered from mountains
in a long walk.

He is a clown, trickster, shaman and priest
a contrary walking backwards
in a circle that never meets.

He is fire and earth, wind and water
doing battle for mother corn maidens
and prairie mystics carrying short pipes.

He is a long pipe wrapped in sage,
smoke rising through clouds and sun dancing
in places where only warriors walk.

He is you, little Johnny.
He is brother to Thunder;
protector of earth flesh

He is laughter rippling
dancing on waves of light.

He knows you little, Johnny
He makes you laugh at your
until you dissolve
into the sounds of tinkling bells.

He scares you out of yourself
to become a fool with no clothes
naked and vulnerable until
you reach
for the earth to find:
      a new face
         a new voice
            a new covering
               for your name.

She

for Sunrise and Cloud Woman

She is the mother of sky
covering open land
bathed in light.

She is the daughter of sun
dancing on snowy horizons
covered in ice crystals and horses' breath.

She is the sun of sons
riding hard on cold ground
wrapped in whiteness and ice.

She is the grandmother
of crow dogs and bears
sleeping in hollows, covered in night.

She is Earth travelling in clouds,
dancing in sun, riding on horses
of blue and red and black and white.

She is trickster, clown, shaman and witch,
hiding in dresses and lace,
panty hose and high heels.

She is you, Sunrise and Cloud woman
tiny girls watching the sky, counting stars
and double rainbows round the moon.

She is as innocent as you,
as old, as wise, as young
Her brown / blue / grey eyes
dance when thunder comes.

She knows Sunrise and Cloud woman

She knows all the little girls
whose eyes are old and laughing
with primal fire
deep in Earth.

She knows.

He and She are Dancers

He is pretty boy, dressed in feathers
and long fur fringes on his braids;
thick braids so shiny
they dance at his waist.
Thick braids and furled feathers
moving rhythmically to drums
and singers singing high notes
through open lips.

She is calm girl, dressed in
a long dress of coloured cotton,
jingling with tiny bells. Thick hair rippling like waves,
tied with wrapped feathers fluttering
in the wind of dance.
Her fine feet draw earth force.
Full earth sounds resonate through
her female body,
fondling sky, like rain fondles earth.

He and She are Dancers
weaving words like songs
through their bodies,
healing sins like sun heals earth,

He and She are Dancers
brother / sister
husband / wife
lovers entwined
the two in one
The one in two
Primal forces fecund with life;
demanding life.

He is a dancer,
beating the earth with hungry feet
taking earth force.

She is a dancer,
crown open to sky force
hungry eye accepting sky
like parched earth accepts rain.

He and She are Dancers
Pretty boy and calm girl;
sated,
full.

August Heat

Auntie died after Christmas.
She lay in the band hall,
her strong brown hands
meeting over her ample lap.

Those hands made the best
Saskatoon berry pie.
All the ladies of the four bands
agreed
no one could match her skill.

Auntie guarded her berry patch
up on the south hill.
Under the poplars
shaded from the hottest sun
those berries grew fat.

Auntie made it so
carrying water up by her
own strong back and her
iron will alone.

In August when the crows
flocked in the trees and
bears meandered down
from the bush country,
Auntie knew she had to share
those purple jewels
hanging heavy
ready to bow to the weight
of bear's paws and sticky fingered
children picking and eating.

Picking and eating
til lips and teeth turned blue
and purple tongues grew thick
on the blooded prairie sun
shine of purple berries
popping.

When the bears and children
ate their fill, Auntie
picked her pails full;
some to freeze for winter dances
and some to bake in pies.

This was Auntie
loving us,
her sweat running off the
ends of her braids
as she bent over her oven
in the late August heat
while thunder rumbled
over the hills.

These were her pies:
      crystallized sugar dusting
      crust that melted
      in our mouths
      mixing with the sweet berry
      juice of Saskatoons
      baked tender with her
      fire and tindered pride.

And when she was sung into the earth
the dogs howled and ran
to the other side
to guide her home.

This Knowledge

The old man
sits in the cloudy sunlight
content
to let the day unfold
as it will.

His gnarled hands
speak of a life
well spent in contemplation
of matters more profound
than material.

His eyes are ancient
older than many lifetimes.
He speaks to me
the young one
impatient to be off.

"This knowledge comes in many ways.
Quietly sometimes
in the whisper
of a butterfly's wings,
or the rustling of the grasses
blown by the winds...

It can come quickly
        in a flash so fast
                you
may miss it
    a single bolt of lightning
        in a silent   humid
        sky.

It can come slowly
        piece by piece
            over the years
                    ...partly revealed
in the markings of a feather
        then on to a misty
half remembered dream
            leading to
voices in a waterfall
barely heard
just barely heard.
Those are the times
that try an old man's soul.
You, too, my girl?"

We watch raindrops
on the window pane
The wind is knocking
a tree branch
against the house.

Somewhere
a clock is ticking
then
silenced   drowned
by the sound
of our beating hearts.

His Bundle

His bundle is full
   of living Earth
      and old stars
         in new time.

A precious bundle replete
   with healing songs and wise stones
      teaching new ways of seeing old things.

His bundle dances in new clothes
   made of old stars and desert flowers
      sewn with cloth woven from white sand
         spun meta-magically.

His bundle is decorated
   with crystals casting rainbows
      over living fringes of red willow
         bending in the wind.

And where he walks, his bundle walks
humming softly old sounds in new time.

It's All in the Stories

for Dad

It's all in the stories, you say.
Story is metaphor,
your round head nods.

It's not about male nor female.
That's not right.
No.
There are no words for
he or she.

And you grin
knowing
your feminist daughter
likes that sort of thing.

It's all there in the stories,
you repeat
and somewhere rabbit
tricks Keewatin yet again.

The thunder tree
shelters the innocent
while horses paint stars
on flanks and withers
and kind old man buffalo
turns to stone.

Story is like a dance -
a metaphor for life
and it's always a different dance.

You understand?

The knotted hairs
gather metaphor and symbol
archetype   and context,
They store them in hankies
and tea cans
under the bed
or back of the house.

They're always gathering
new ways to make
things clear.

Don't listen to the people who
say the stories have to be told
exactly the way they're
given to you.

That rule was made for
anthropologists
who didn't understand
the stories come from down here.

You touch your belly and you grin.

If you feel it, you can tell it.

Write it down.
Make a poem.
Make a video.
There's always new ways
to tell a good story.

Someday my grandchildren
will use computer animation
or virtual reality.

The stories won't die my girl.
As long as we tell them
they'll live.

Invasion

Beginnings

In the late summer of 1989, I sat with my brother and sister-in-law in their lodge. Something was not right with my children. I was worried for their future, hoping that I could unlock the mystery of their unhappiness.

As we prayed I moved into dream. Darkness swirled. I saw my sons in the bedroom of our Vancouver home. They cowered in the lower bunk. Over and over, my older son cried, "We're too little. We're too little." The man raped them warning that if they told me, I would no longer love them. Their terror was pitiful. Sick, leaden and heavy, I gasped for breath. I cried, "All my relations!" and the sweat lodge door opened.

The realization that my sons were defiled so deeply was almost beyond comprehension. I sat rocking in shock. I felt the vision deep inside. I wailed and cried and cried and cried. All became so clear to me. I sat with my brother until nearly midnight crying and talking, crying and talking.

****

How do you heal a family?
How do you find the words to speak the unspeakable?
This Red Moon has taken fourteen years to write.
As I sit here at my computer, my belly tied in knots
I struggle to control my breath.

Where would I find the help I needed to heal my wounded family? Would my boys have the courage to face the truth? Many aboriginal people all over the country are talking about sexual abuse. I know enough to know that each person heals in his or her own time. There could be no forcing it with my sons. I confided in a dear friend and medicine man who told me forcefully without equivocation that the very best thing I could do for my sons was to take care of myself first. What was it that I most wanted to do?

The sweat lodge provided me with my answer. At the end of the third round of a particularly hot and difficult sweat, the door was opened and a coyote peeked inside. She titled her head and she smiled! She turned and trotted south. "Hey John!" I gasped to my brother. "Did you see that coyote?" He smiled and looked inscrutable. We finished the fourth round. I crawled out of the lodge. I heard a voice say "University of Arizona - the old stories."

I came to in Tucson in the fall of 1990. I and my twelve year old son Luke moved to the desert. I worked on a Masters in Creative Writing. N. Scott Momaday was teaching oral traditions. Joy Harjo was my mentor and reinforced the truth my words were more than me. I loved the desert. I loved school. I loved the one hundred other writers in the program. I was not alone.

Luke was not so lucky. The landscape confused him. He couldn't figure out the rules at school. The kids were different. I drove him every day for two weeks. I had the uneasy feeling that his travelling on the school bus would be problematic. Finally, we decided the day had come to ride the long yellow school bus. That afternoon, when it was time to go home, Luke walked out the wrong door and couldn't find his bus. Deciding that it wasn't too far to home, Luke began to walk. It was 110 degrees. He had no water. No idea he was walking the wrong way.

At 5:30, I called the police. They chided me for not calling them sooner. I was surprised they would take this disappearance seriously. They were wonderful. I was shocked. Within twenty minutes, two members of a special family unit knocked on my door. After questioning me, they decided Luke was not a runaway. They asked for a picture and a detailed description. A search was mounted. Night fell. Helicopters crisscrossed the sky. I was contacted every half hour to see if Luke had made it home. As time passed, all available cars were called into the search. I became more and more afraid that some perverted sadist had abducted my boy or worse. At 9:30, a policeman phoned to see if Luke had arrived home yet. He informed me they were going to call out the National Guard!

No Canadian cops would bother searching for one missing Indian kid until at least 24 hours had passed and even then you'd have to bang your shoe to get some action. Now the National Guard! Five minutes later, a cop phoned. Luke had been found. He had gone into a convenience store to get a drink of water and the cashier, knowing that a boy matching his description was missing, had phoned the police. After that night, Luke began to unravel and slid slowly, slowly.

****

The boy huddled, hands swollen by the hundreds of puncture wounds made by the cactus as he picked the ripe fruit. His mouth scarlet like a baby suckling a blood filled breast. The boy was silent. He had seen his death and there was nothing more to say. He knew now that time had curved in on itself. He had always known it was possible. He thought about his mother's blue car and knew he was not of that time. The desert stretched untouched by roads, smog, or any thing man made. He wondered who his mother was. He became lonely, so terribly lonely. Exhausted, he had never felt so tired. He remembered running and running through the streets - a stranger in a stranger land. He had not belonged to that hot desert city. The cactus, the heat, the noise of the helicopters, the dryness did not belong to him. He was terrified as the black jeep came closer and closer, the expression on the dark man's face. Who would believe him? Who would ever understand the darkness of the fear? "I will hide from my death. I will become a seed until my mother find me, then I will live again."

****

The red fruit rotted into the sand. Inside the black seed the boy felt the terrors. He made himself very, very small. He had tried to describe the terrors to his mother but he had no words then, not even now. The dark came nearer and nearer. He ran and he ran - down the concrete path, he ran screaming, the knife raised overhead dripping. Somewhere far away he could hear his mother calling.

"Luke! Luke! Don't hurt the babies."

September 26, 1991. The sky was pink and the later afternoon light made everything magical. That's what I remember as I ran after Luke. Golden light bounced off the toddlers innocent faces as they played in the coolness of the setting sun. They laughed and gurgled at the strange silly boy who ran through their play area. Luke's eyes stared out of his head as he ran with the big knife. One of his friends ran along beside him calmly talking to him. "Luke, your mother wants you to bring her knife back. She needs it to cook dinner. You'd like to eat dinner wouldn't you? Come on Luke, why don't you let me carry the knife?" Luke lost him in the desert that bordered the university housing site.

****

The boy crouched on the gray rock perched high on the hill. The sky shone blood through the trees, shadows roared. He cowered under their hands and teeth, smothered under their will. Shadows taunted him. Voices roared. "No one is going to love you now." The boy drowned in the noise and the fading light of the blood.

****

Luke was no longer in his body. Knuckles cracked and bloody. Kids on the ward kept away from him. He pounded walls, doors, his body, his head. I searched his eyes, some sign that my boy was there. He growled, averted his eyes. All I read was shame.

I had been going to the hospital every day, sometimes twice a day if my schedule permitted. Luke began to threaten me. "I could kill you right now," he'd say and I believed those eyes. My boy was gone and something malevolent had taken his place. Finally, the Doctor asked me to stop visiting. The treatment team wanted to see if my absence might shock Luke back to reality. It didn't work. Luke got worse. A few days later, the family councilor called to tell me that Luke was locked in the padded room and put on 24 hour watch. This meant that someone would sit in the room with him continually until he broke or until he required medication.

At my request, I was allowed to talk to him. I wanted to let him know that though I wouldn't be at the hospital, I would be thinking about him. As I was buzzed through a series of locked doors leading to the holding room, I thought about how different Luke's stay in psychiatric care was than mine had been twenty-five years before. Luke would never have electroshock "therapy." I looked through the one-way window into my son's holding room, I was relieved to see that the padded walls were white not gray and he was not buckled. The man who sat on the floor with him looked kind and compassionate. Our family therapist stood with me. "Luke will never be left alone. This worker will stay with him night and day for four days. He's our most experienced councilor and he has worked with Luke's Doctor many times before. Your son has the very best care this hospital has to offer. He's a very sick boy."

I knew that I could not speak to Luke. He was too far away to hear. The next ninety-six hours were interminable to me. I went to class. I did my reading. I couldn't write. I barely ate. I prayed continually. I begged. I bargained. I demanded. I wept. I tried to find my Luke.

What kind of torture does a human being experience when he is scared out of himself? What do the voices tell him in his terror? I thought about Luke's road to that padded room. Someone must have totally terrified him somewhere, sometime. Was my vision true in the sweat lodge? And what of my other son Steven who wore the pain on his face and in the sinews and bones of his body. My brain didn't want to acknowledge such a heinous act but my soul knew it was true.

Would the land be strong enough to call my Luke back or would his terror keep him safe in his insanity?

Three days into Luke's sojourn in the padded room, a fellow poet and wise woman phoned. She was in Tucson to do a reading. "Tomorrow at ten I'll be in my hotel room. I've arranged some time and some help to find Luke. You stay home alone and tomorrow morning I want you to anchor me as I go out in search of him. He needs to be reminded that he chose this life. He has an obligation to live it."

The next morning I did as she instructed. That afternoon at four o'clock, I got a phone call from the hospital. "Luke is back. He wants to start working at therapy. He'd like to see you." I jumped in my car and drove to the hospital stopping along the way to pick up a helium filled balloon which said, "Welcome back."

I shall always remember the look on his face as he lopped down the hospital corridor to greet me. He had a long road to walk but at least he had chosen to walk the road.

****

Luke was born unusual. He thought way beyond the usual parameters of boydom. One day when he was four, he told me that he lay awake long after every one else in the house was asleep. "I used to do that too," I said, "I used to count the stars and wonder about the meaning of infinity." Luke replied, "Oh mom that's easy. Time and the stars end where God lives."

Luke was always thinking about the meaning of reality and the nature of time. One day toward the end of grade one, Luke came home and said, "You know mom, people who think in straight lines just don't see how the line curves. Our thoughts make what we think is reality. But reality is bigger than our thoughts." Luke drew complex diagrams. He talked of permeable membranes and time curving in on itself. He said we could move forward and backward in time and everything influenced everything else.

One day Luke found an old golf ball and cut it open. Something clicked and Luke found his golf ball model of time. This is how he explained it to me: "The elastic string represents time. You stretch the elastic and time passes instantaneously. The elastic string is wound around and around making a ball which is covered with a permeable membrane. That's Earth. All the people walk on the string. Everyone's thoughts travel on the string. Some people can put their ears to the string and that is how they know what is happening in other places without listening to the news on T.V. The string overlaps; I am standing on one part of the string and you on another part and our places on the string touch. We share the same reality for a time.

"Now picture this Mom. The ball is spinning and it's travelling through the universe. Everything in space moves on a curve and eventually makes circles, thousands of circles within circles. As our ball moves along, energy flows through the permeable membrane. Some people can hook into the energy of the universe. Other people can't see farther than the little bit of string that they stand on. They're squished in the middle of the ball but they don't realize it.

"Now you think that words are energy. Everything we say travels along the string. Positive energy helps the ball spin properly and negative energy works against it. Sometimes the string gets tangled up and things go wrong. World War Two was a big tangle in the string. Six million Jews were killed and we've been spending the time ever since trying to unravel the tangles in the string."

****

Though Luke's psychiatrist argued for more time and money to treat Luke, my brother Doug lobbied in Canada for more funding, by mid November we ran out of options. Medical Health Services would no longer fund Luke's care in the States. They argued that he could be treated adequately in Saskatchewan and wanted to transfer Luke by air ambulance to the University Hospital in Saskatoon. Luke was making progress and I was desperate to protect his safety. I knew that a transfer to a new environment would harm his progress because he had only recently come back and he trusted his Doctor, therapist and other care givers on the ward. The idea of a stranger taking my son home bothered me. Luke was too fragile and fearful to be placed in the hands of strangers. I feared he might regress to the dark world that he had just left.

I phoned Saskatchewan Health and made a deal: give my son two more weeks and I will personally drive him home. They agreed. I talked to the department head of my program at the university and we worked out a plan so that I could complete my MFA in Saskatchewan. A faculty member was assigned to work with me by mail and phone. Though I didn't realize it, I was severely stressed. I was running on adrenaline and nothing else. The two weeks flew by as I finished the requirements for the semester, I visited daily at the hospital, packed what I could and sold the rest of our household goods.

****

I was not ready to leave Tucson. I loved going to school. The students and staff of my program were unfailingly supportive as I wrestled with the demons plaguing my son. I loved the desert and the fierce thunder and lightning that raced down the mountains every evening during the monsoons. My spirit didn't want to leave but it had to be so for my son.

As we drove through the desert past Phoenix on the road to Las Vegas, I tried to keep my son calm. He was so ill and I was so tired. As we neared Winslow I began to see double. I was nauseous and sweaty. I had to stop but the road was narrow and the traffic heavy. Then on the right side of the road, I saw a roadside cantina where we pulled in and stopped. I held on to the steering wheel and prayed the pain in my head would subside and that Luke would be able to go into the cantina with me. Finally I said, "Luke I have a very bad headache and I feel sick. I need you to be very brave now and come into the cantina with me so I can rest." With an effort, Luke focused on my face. "Mom, your face is gray. Don't worry, I will try very hard to be with people and if it gets too hard, I'll come back to the car."

The cantina was divided: an adult drinking section and a place for families with children whose parents perhaps wanted some brew with their enchiladas. The walls were covered with every rattle snake product: rattler key chains, rattler hat bands, rattle chess pieces, stuffed rattlers of every size and shape, rattler coasters, rattler boots, rattler fangs preserved in plastic with the words: "Winslow, Arizona Rattle Snake Capital of the World." Luke and I sat down at the table close to the door. We looked at each other and laughed. "Luke, are you ok with this?" "Just as long as they're all dead," he replied. Then he went back into his world of safety. I wished I could go into mine. Though I had been sober for fourteen years I thought of ordering a brew - something to take the edge but we would never have made it home and we had such a long road.

I dug around in my bag and found a dusty aspirin. I ate a good meal and Luke was very brave as he struggled to stay with me. He ate very little but we managed to rest.

Sometimes it is grace and only grace that carries us along and that evening it was grace that gave us the sun setting in all its glorious majesty over Las Vegas as we began our accent into the mountains. Bright yellows, oranges and reds bathed the valley as deep purples and indigos moved in from the east. "Good-bye desert, good-bye," Luke sang to the hills.

We made it to St. George, Utah that night where we stayed at a clean little motel. The owners were very kind. I think they realized we were no ordinary travellers. Luke went right to bed and I took some time to smoke and gaze at the bright stars. I could not drive all the way home without help. I called my dad and asked him to meet us in Salt Lake. He arrived by plane at two the next day.

I mailed three boxes of books in Salt Lake to make room for an extra passenger and Dad took us out for a steak dinner. Food has always been extremely important to Luke. Even when he was a little kid he loved to open cupboards and admire all the food and when supplies got low he would get anxious until the cupboards were filled. My sister said he must have starved in another life. Of all the food that Luke likes, steak, "charred on the outside, medium on the inside," is his favorite. Dad knew just what to do to distract Luke from his growing anxiety.

After the waiter had taken our order, Luke became agitated. My father said, "Luke, focus on this." Dad leaned over the table and presented his nose upon which sat a large red pimple.

Luke looked closely. "Grandpa, does it hurt?" "Not very," said Grandpa, "but isn't it ugly?" Luke contemplated the pimple then began to laugh. "It sure is Grandpa." So every time Luke became anxious as we ate we would examine Grandpa's pimple.

We made it through dinner and bunked down for the night: Dad across the hall and Luke and I sharing a large room with two beds. Luke was exhausted but every time he fell asleep he soon woke from a nightmare. Sometimes he would get up and try to open the door. He was sleep walking and terrified. Once he walked down the corridor crying for Grandpa. I persuaded him to return to our room but he was afraid to sleep alone. "Mama, will you sleep with me?"

I wrapped my baby tightly and held him to my heart. "It's ok Luke, you're safe, you're safe," I crooned as I rocked him into a troubled sleep.

Many times over the years I have marveled at Luke's courage; then as he struggled to maintain his tenuous ties to reality and all the days since when the shadows touch him and call his name.

****

The way home was a dream unfolding. Snow dusted the November land but no storm blew in to hinder our way. I remember the sight of Saskatchewan from the Bear Hills and the feeble winter sun through snow. At the border the biting wind whipped as a young border guard tried to determine if we were smuggling an American car. Dad appealed to his compassion: "We have a very sick boy here."

We made it home. A storm blew in. Luke went to the hospital.

Over the years, many people have judged me for the

way I have "allowed" Luke to be treated for his mental illness. Some have denied that he is "really" sick. A psychologist once told me he was "just a bad boy." Recovering alcoholics recoil when they discover he is prescribed "mood altering drugs" saying they would never take them under any circumstances. Some traditionalists insist doctoring would cure him, others insist he suffers from a spiritual illness that can be healed with the right intervention from a spiritual healer. Medical practitioners insist that he suffers from a biochemical disorder of the brain. Others minimize his situation saying it's just a case of him taking his meds—no problem, he gets well, goes back to school and gets a job.

Then there are the rarities: the wise, mostly women who reassure me, support me and uphold the sacred ties between children and mothers. They tell me to follow my intuition, trust my knowing, pray, heal myself and I will heal my children. They make the most sense to me.

This Red Moon

for Steven with Love

Tonight
the moon is a hard red disk.

Passpassces predicted it would be so.

Your Grandpa told me the Old Man
fasted for twelve days
with my Great-Grandfather, Missatimos
at Manito Lake
the time of the
hungry pup when the people
were starving and fearful.

Passpassces dreamed and saw many things.

"The people shall suffer a long war," he said.

Passpassces knew
        in this red moon
flowed the memories;

        groping hands in the night,
        children crying
        keeping secrets too,
        too shamed to know

        it was not their fault.

        black whirlwinds
        inside their souls
        men   beating women, they
        mirrored their own self   hate

        children watching

thinking terror is life
and love   too bloody to risk

Passpassces saw   the black water
invading our sacred spaces,
drowning our knowing that
life is to be lived
and love is what heals

Our relations cried
in their love   in their love
for   our red clay
blood
cradled in our land
covered in sky.

In that night they called
creation
and they smoked and prayed.

Passpassces held the pipe
wept and shivered for
the ache of our starving
and the confusion of memory
hardened to shame.

"This red moon tell us
the way back to life will be
by doing battle   inside ourselves.

This will not be war as we have known it:
many will die in the fight
many will run from the blood letting
many will hide in the black water
many will try to escape the color of their skin

But

 More will claim their warrior blood
 more will pray their road to peace
 more will dance under the thunderers' nest
 more will sing their way to freedom
 more will make their marks on paper
 in the spirit telling of all this
 that we pray for those not yet born."

Passpassces fell silent
people murmured amongst themselves
fearful
not knowing if we would find the courage
nor even recognize the war

"How will we survive?" they cried.
(meaning all of us for seven generations to come)

How will we survive?

There's no way forward
but through
this red moon blood
memory
and the telling of   it, son.

And the victory.

And the victory.

Slow Burn

Slow burn   you and I,
tectonic plates grinding
fire rising through the
fault.

You?
You will listen to me now!

You in your priest robes and
churchly platitudes.

You will listen to me now!

Your godly words disguised
a man-child burning
a man so twisted
child rape was justified
as good for the soul

beating the young
of their sin was
atonement.

Suffering.

You never understood it.

      Putting on the black suit,
      the god collar
      you were no longer
      responsible.

      What is god's work then?

Slow burn   you and I

You old man-child,
under your god's collar
you carried a bundle of
in righteousness
thinking it would
protect you from yourself,
the heat of your denial
wormed through your soul.

Your fire consumed you
burning away the guts
and flesh
and blood
of hands and
genitals that beat
on the innocent
flailed their way
to the godless places
where children's
screams were choked
and child bodies succumbed
to you!

You!

Children ran and hid;

        a godless man in god's clothes
        pompously judging our worth.

You!

How many others were
left

thinking:

> *My body betrays me.*
> *God doesn't love children*
> *who have been raped and beaten*
> *by god's man*
>
> *for their own good.*

You!

You twisted truth to salve
your soul   beat and
raped yourself
by anger, hunger
hate and hopelessness:
       roads built on the bones
       of ancestors,
       Yes!
       This was your legacy.
       This!   Child-man:
              A slow burn in the guts
              silence
              wood feeding coals that
              smoldered
              unspoken in you and me.

Was it the winds of memory
that flamed
the conflagration
that consumed you in the end?

I will not inherit your prairie fire.
I will not starve in a sea of grass.

I give it back to you.

Take this pain.
It belongs to you.

Take this guilt.
It's yours.

Take back the stolen years.

Carry them in your burden basket.

Carry the sticks you used
to beat the innocent,
the heavy words you weighted
on our child's flesh.

Carry the priestly clothes
you used to cow the devout.

Carry them now.

All of this
belongs to you.

Seven Songs for Uncle Louie

in the voice of young Louis Riel

In the seminary I pray
until my knees bleed.
St. Joseph doesn't smile
and the Virgin never speaks.

Tache'
he says "Pray, Louis,
you will go far in the Church."

I say the rosary until
my voice is hoarse but
St. Joseph doesn't hear.

Is the patron saint of the Métis
deaf to seminarians?

Tache'
He says I will save the Métis,
it is God's will.

But,
my father fights for the people
and prays infrequently, at least
I do not see his knees bleed.
All he has ever known
is the fight to defend the land
and the liberty of the Métis.

Tache'
he says God listens to the
supplications of lowly seminarians.

Louis Told Me

in the voice of Evelina, Louis' betrothed

Louis told me
> when his father died
> he felt him heave
> his last breath

and though
> he was miles away
> he heard his father say

> Louis David, to you
> I transfer my bundle.
It is small and humble
> wrapping little things
> a bone
> from the last buffalo,
> a stone
> from the Assiniboine,
> a small pipe and tobacco pouch
and,
> a feather
> from the broken wing
> of one who flew too low.

Louis told me
> he couldn't hear the
> burden of that bundle.

And when
> his father died,
> he was alone
> and the voices
> and the phantom winds
> blew
>> his soul
>>> away.

"Evelina, Evelina,
> I have been seeking my
> shadow ever since."

We Orangemen

in the voices of an Orange Lodge chorus

We Orangemen
don't want that mixed-blood,
sullied by the savage
love of wasted land
singing war songs
in our parliament.

He is not one of us.

It is enough for us
that the French presume
equality with the blood
of our Empire
blessed by God and Queen.

No

Not Riel, uncivilized half-man
murderer of Brother Scott,
never will he sit with
the true men of Britannia.

We Orangemen know
what is best to bless
this new land:
        Our God, white and right
        to cleave away the wanton
        blood of darkness
        riding long enough
        from us.

        No   Not Riel.

That Anglais They Say

in the voice of Louis Riel

That anglais they say
I am crazy
the francophone   and the Métis.

But you old man
Why   do you smile?

Because you are gifted, Louis,
with second sight   like me.

But you   are not a man.
They   do not perceive
you   as such.
You   are a savage
who drifts
    over crosses
and churches
        and votive candles.

Louis, learn to use this gift.
    Smoke your pipe and wear your sash.
If I am gifted
        as you say

Why?
   do you   allow me
   to suffer?

Why
   do you turn   into silent
            wings
      that disappear
      in the night?

When at Last I Found Him

in the voice of Gabriel Dumont

When at last I found him
      kneeling in the church
He was enraptured
      deep
      in communion
      with the One Above.

Tears
      engulfed him
Even   when the sun
stepping free
      from the clouds
      enveloped him
        with light.

And when he turned to us, I
      stepped forward enjoining him
      Louis, come home.
They cry out and no one listens.
      They die and no one sees.

He came with us
      and near the Bear Paw hills,
I saw him gaze over them
      with such foreboding
      I entreated him to explain.

"I see a hangman's noose
suspended from the clouds

We Came To Fight

in the voice of Sailing Horse, Cree war chief

We came to fight
with Louis at Batoche.
It was in the time
of the hungry pup
when our people
were dying
daily
of starvation and disease.

We had nothing left to lose
by fighting with our nistas.
Their fight was ours
because they were our relations.

We smoked together and
   Louis had a vision
   that we would be victorious
   under a clouded sky.

I wondered how it would be possible
   when we were so few
   with nothing left to eat
   nor bullets for our guns.

But I saw nothing.
How could I question
a man's vision from the One Above?

Dumont pleased with Louis
   "Let the Indian sharp shooters
   go out and harry the troops.
   Let them pick off the leaders
   one by one."

But Louis was resolute.
      "We must be civilized men of war."

Middleton's army marched
to the sound of music
foreign to the voice
of the prairie wind and
      we want our honor songs
      to veterans of other wars.

For a moment our voices blended
      with Middleton's musical march
and with the voice of the wind
older than hungry pups or
civilized men until,

the army charged.

I tried to protect Louis
as I ran from cover to cover
shooting carefully at the redcoats.
My bear cub robe would protect me
if I wasn't foolish.
      But Louis and his God's cross
      seemed stronger than my Bear,
      at least, I thought so
      then.

Standing naked, in full view of the enemy
Louis prayed loudly, his voice carrying
      over the sounds of their
      Gatling gun
      cannons and rifles
      and the pitiful wails of the women.

Louis held his God's cross aloft
admonishing us to fight on.

We shot nails and stones
and buttons
ripped from the coats of
children.

And when the battle was lost,
        the sun clouded over
        and we fled,
        running for our lives.

        They say that when the
        Redcoats took Louis
        he was wearing only
        a ragged sash
        and carried his God's cross
        broken in his hands.

Fire and Ice

for Brian Mulroney from all of us.

Who was guilty of this breach of
natural law?

Who can say what love lead us to this,
what hate, what passionate lack of
faith.

Was it you whose fear overwhelmed
your best intentions?
Or was it my desire for respect
that daunted your pristine belief
that you knew better than I
what was "realistic" or "bizarre?"

How could you know
living as you did
in that cabin by the lake
with your Canadian Club and soda
mixed in that cold crystal glass,
that you were not
in the best of shape
to judge?

Whose delusions brought us
to this madness?
Whose voice unleashed
the rifles and the tear gas,
the cigarette burns
and the stones that broke
an old man's heart?

Don't tell me
you're prepared to listen if
I'll just behave.

Don't tell me
that time and patience
will heal these wounds.

Don't harbor your delusions, sir,
that ice will cool
this fire
that rages in my gut.

Quarto de Luna

1.   Dark Moon

Body memorizes   voices caught
in the throats of wolves.
Wind echoes through this
forest of night terrors and mind sweats.
The heart hum dies in this
cacophony
          punched walls and torn flesh
          harsh words tracing
          phantoms imprinted
          on skin too thin
          to take the line.

I walk away from this:
pinched nerves, taut mouths,
thin lies that cut
this dark blood soaked moon.

2.   Emerging Moon

To take this chance and
love   again,

who knows where this will   lead us
except, perhaps, to
light?

3.   Full Moon

The sky swells, fondled by
reflected light dancing
shadows on your skin.

What ancient force is this
that calls us home to feast
once more?

We will love this moon together,
two spirits rising in its light.

Once more   we whisper
urgent declarations
          "I love you."
          "I love you."
once more
              despite this war
              for love.

4.   Retreating Moon

for survivors in their desperation
love   too much
            too soon
            too fully out of need
            to quickly fill the void
            left by another who came and went

I retreat from this,
behind the veil of
earth   the dark side of the moon.

enchanted by the solitude
of night   too young to be old
              too old to lust

In between,   the survivors
of child rape and broken mothers
scurry for cover.

Four Songs for the Fifth Generation

Drums, chants, and rattles
pounded earth and
> *heartbeats*
> *heartbeats*

"They were our life   the life
> of the prairies
We loved them
> and they loved us.
Sometimes   they were so many
they flowed   like a river
over the hills   into the valleys.

I saw them.   I knew them.
I helped my mother
> cut away their skin
> chop their bones
and dry their meat
> Many times
> many times.

Aye, but now,   they are gone
> ghosts   all ghosts.

The sickness came
> we were hungry
I saw my children   die
one by one
one by one.

There was no freedom   then my girl
> They were stronger
> They thought they knew
what it was   their God wanted.

Aye, but now   they are gone
        ghosts   just ghosts.

Sometimes   I think I hear
their thunder   smell their dust
at night my girl
        at night I dream
dream of their warm blood
        their hides covering
Aye, covering   all my children
    in their sleep."

Drums, chants and rattles
pounded earth and
        heartbeats
        heartbeats.

"That's the old Simmons homestead.
            He's dead now
I don't know what happened
        to his wife   and children.

Back in the thirties
        we cut posts for him
10 cents a post   that was good money
            back then.
Clarence Simmons was his name
        came from England
            with his skinny little wife
and a bunch of pale scrawny little kids.

Poor Simmons   we felt sorry for him
        so we helped him
            as much as we could.

Back in the thirties,
things weren't so bad for us
            as it was for the homesteaders
We hadn't cut our trees
        or tore up the land.
            We still had deer
                and fish
                    rabbits
and gophers and fat dogs
                    heh heh

But the settlers really suffered.
            It was pitiful.
My dad would tell us
        "take this meat over to the Simmons
    place. Drop it at the door."

So I'd ride over   real quiet
    and hang it by the house

Poor Simmons
            one day he hung himself
                from a tree
                    in his yard.
Couldn't take it no more.
            Dad found him,
            cut him down
and laid him   real gentle
            on the ground
                under the tree.

That was one of the few times
    I ever saw him cry.

I don't know what makes
        some men
            go on living
while other men
        give up.

Drums, chants and rattles
pounded earth and
            heartbeats
            heartbeats.

"It was 1960
            when dad and mom
                got the vote.
All us kids got copies of Canada's
        'Declaration of Human Rights'
and took them home
            and put them up
                all over the walls.
Yeah, that was a great day
for Canada
        'Oh, Canada'
        Our true north strong and free."

We moved south when I was ten
        to a town with sidewalks
        and running water
and playground with a pool,
        not a lake
'Hey, Injuns!   Yer not allowed
        in the pool.
You'll get it dirty.
            dirty.'

We closed ranks after that
        spent a lot of time
        exploring the creek.

My brother found an arrowhead
    Some white kid said
    it didn't belong to us,
so my brother beat him up.

My brother was always
                fighting
        It seemed
    he had a rage
    that wouldn't go out.
Me,   I just retreated
    and retreated
        until I couldn't
        find myself.

There was a boy down the street
    who had it in
        for my brother
        called him dirty Indian.
He'd sick his dog on him
        every time
        we'd walk to school.

We took to walking the long way
    everyone   except my brother.

One time my brother hit that dog
    smack between the eyes
            with a rock
The old dog tucked his tail
    between his legs and
    went howling off
        behind the house.

The boy came to our place
　　with a baseball bat
We were all going to go out
　　and kick that kid around,
but Dad said 'No
　　let your brother
　　fight it out."

They were pretty evenly matched
　　　the kid with his bat,
　　my brother with his stones.
　　　　They fought
　　　　for an hour

kicking
hitting
scratching
punching
thwacking
ripping

Mom wanted to stop them
　　　but Dad said no.
　　　'He's got to take a stand.'

Finally it was over
　　　nobody won.

That kid never sicked
　　his dog on my brother again.
　　　　but
my brother's rage
never did go away.

Drums, chants and rattles
pounded earth and
        heartbeats
        heartbeats

"I don't want to go
        to a white high school
                Mama.
My spirit would die
        in a place like that
I love our little school
        us Indians
        we help each other.
                We care.
We share smokes, Mom.

When I grow up
will my kids
have to fight
for a place in the neighbourhood
too?"

Drums, chants and rattles
pounded earth and
        heartbeats
        heartbeats.

Compañera Indigena

for Alberto Perez Esquivel

You know the agony of flaying skin and broken bone,
Day/night   infinite sleeplessness.

Electric currents of   hate writhing in the abyss.
Hidden voices saying

          "You will submit."
                    "You will submit."

In the mind warp of   the netherworld
you glimpse the beast lurking.

          You resist.

  You resist.

In that brutal darkness,   spirit sings
      deep song   cradled with steel
        burnished by love
stronger than the insanity
              of military might.

Their mind sweep
          destroys the soul of Argentina

          Almost
but for the companeros,   You who are fed
by something more   than the destroyers will ever
          understand.

You live, mey compañera Indigena.

You live to spread the fire,
ignite the passion of these simple truths:
                We are companions of the heart.
                The land will always own us.

        Yes.

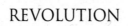

REVOLUTION

In the Firelight

I am alone in the firelight
(homework's done, kids asleep)
wondering if I will ever be held
by a strong man, warm heart.
I am alone in the firelight adding up the bills
(the rent cheque bounced today)
wondering what it's like to live
in a two-income family,
wondering what it's like to be
sometimes a passenger, not always a driver,
wondering what it's like to share the cooking
to share a life.

I am alone in the firelight
(gotta get more wood)
wondering what I've got that they don't got:
less meat to buy
less washing up
less laundry to fold
less toilet paper and shampoo for sure
more freedom to go places
more walls to paint
more walks to shovel
more time to read
more time to write
more time to sit alone in the fire light
wondering if I will ever be held
(is the cat in? did I lock the door?)

Married Man

Don't tempt me charmer
take your snake and flute away.
Don't flash those baby browns at me.
Take those eyes and liquid lips
home to your sandy brown wife,
your cute kids and your damn cows.

Don't park your lizard boots
by my bed charmer.
Take your wind and earth smells
home to the farm and
the son-of-a-bitchin' harvest moon.

Don't press that smooth brown skin on mine.
Don't murmur those sounds, not words,
I may think for one moment
that I can feed the cows with you
and live with wind and earth

forever.

Don't tempt me.
Don't let me hear the flute song.
Don't let me feel the snake;
hard as stone.
I will be driven down, buried cold,

alone.

Don't tempt me charmer.
I can't give you
a temporary home for stone.
There's nothing in the harvest moon
but family, church and cows:
your sandy brown wife wondering
why you're late;
your children asking where's daddy,
and those cows, bawling for their feed.

Green beneath the Willow

Green beneath the willow
            Waves broken on shore
sun dances   leaves fetid in the rain.

There is no vision here
        of transformation
no consciousness   rising

alone

under pines

        needles break   breath

Breath is here   life

Just life.

If I could have one day in the prairie sun,
        a day with you.

Eating apples and plotting our way west,
        we would choose the roads we will travel
        on the way to the rest of our life.

Just a breath past the world's largest Easter Egg,
        the Dairy Queen will call and you will take
        photos of me nose deep in a small cone.

Just blocks from the West Edmonton Mall,
        my intestines will scream   stop!
        and you scramble yet again
        to find an open john   a garage, a convenience store
        anywhere

anywhere.

Anywhere with you would be better than here.

    give me a vision
let it be the prairie wind   even at forty below.
    even in the raging hail storm   clouds swirling overhead

    give me a vision
let it be the northern pines   cracking in the heat
    of wild fires   even that   even that

is more than   leaves rotting the undergrowth.

Shake 'N Bake

He wore the uniform of the lowly
like a cop wears a gun and a badge;
worn blue jeans neatly patched
by his woman of the moment,
and a humble shirt of plaid flannel
muted and discreet
Oh so discreet.

And when he went to advise the lowly
he played his somber medicine man voice
turned up the base, lowered the treble
and cleared his throat
Yes, always cleared his throat.

He talked as though he were barely literate
and he had just learned English last week.
He didn't like to read
and would sometimes take two whole days
to finish *Black Elks Speaks* or
Selected Studies in Native American Shamanism

He would talk ever so discreetly
about "the others"
the shake 'n bake medicine men
who didn't know what they were doing
and didn't deserve to do it anyway.
Yes, they were so wrong and they
would be sorry.

"There is so much to teach people"
he would say. "So much has been lost.
You've got to watch the old guys, even
the old people have forgotten. It's sad,"
he would say, clearing his throat
"the way those young people go to them."

But he knew the score. He was real.
He had *earned* the right to do what he did.
Every summer he took great pains
to fast at someone else's expense
and performed the requisite ceremonies
diligently and correctly.
So correctly.

There was no one whom he trusted
and no one whom he loved.
He rarely really laughed. He would
tell crude jokes to the boys
but always made sure
he was pure before
he performed a
ceremony.
for this
was the way
he understood
it to be:
    Step 1
    Step 2
    Step 3

Zen Indian

Zen Indian tiptoes into Taos
watches coyote disguised
as an ice-cream vendor
sell dollar popsicles
to thirsty tourists.

Fishes down the Fraser
for dried salmon
thinking a No. 10 hook
will catch those freeze-dried suckers.

Careens into Calgary in time
for Stampede; bells polished
feathers fluffed
to dance three times a day
for a free pass to the rodeo.

Makes it to Winnipeg
just after Bismark and right before
wild rice time
to get folk-sy at the Indian Pavilion

then it's on to pick wild rice
for Uncle Ben;
drop a few rocks in the sacks,
shoot at the crows and reminisce
about how it used to be
before the harvest became
the domain of Bros in hydro
planes and enough money for gas.

Oh oh, cold's coming.
Time to find a fine filly
with a job, not too many kids
and a warm place to lay up for
the winter.

Put cities in a hat:
   Minneapolis, LA
      Boulder, Sante Fe
Calgary, Seattle, Salt Lake.

Yee-ha! Watch out Boulder!
Here he comes.
Zen Indian on the road to enlightenment!

Post-Oka Kinda Woman

Here she comes strutting down your street.
This post-Oka woman don't take no shit.

She's done with victimization, reparation,
degradation, assimilation,
devolution, coddled collusion,
the "plight of the native Peoples."

Post-Oka woman,
She sashay   into your suburbia.
Mackenzie Way, Riel Crescent   belong to her
like software microwave ovens,
plastic Christmas trees and lawn chairs.

Her daughter wears Reeboks and works out.
Her sons cook   and wash up.
Her grandkids don't sass their Kokum!

She drives a Toyota, reads best-sellers,
sweats on week-ends, colors her hair,
sings old songs, gathers herbs.
Two steps Tuesdays
round dances Wednesdays,
twelve steps when she needs it.

Post-Oka woman she's struttin'
not walkin' one step behind her man.
She don't take that shit
Don't need it!   Don't want it!
You want her   then treat her right.

Talk to her of post-modern de-constructivism
She'll say;   "What took you so long?"
You wanna discuss Land Claims?

She'll tell ya she'd rather leave
her kids with a struggle than a bad settlement.

Indian Government?
          Show her cold hard cash.

Tell her you've never talked to a real live Indian.
          She'll say: "Isn't that special."

Post-Oka woman, she's cheeky.
          She's bold.   She's cold,

And she don't take no shit.

No shit!

She Ties Her Bandana

She ties her bandana
swiftly, surely
tightly around her head
containing
all the images, thoughts
and doubts
assailing her.

It is spring.
Soon the Thunderers
will come
out of the west
they will come
      wrapped in their mysteries
      clocked in mist.

Where are the others?
They
   who tie their bandanas
   tightly
Do their eyes
   ache in the last light of the sun?
Do they fear their racing thoughts?
   their memories, their dreams?

She remembers
    a blond haired, blue eyed suitor
    saying
"The prairies make mystics of us all."
    and his naive desire to impress her
    with his sensitivity
    and his innocent expectation
    that by loving her
    he too
    could become "Indian"

But that was long ago
so long ago
it feels like a dream
now
She is alone
and has been for some time
Sometimes she feels
like she had always been alone
and always will be.

Like all the widows
    of all the wars
like all the sisters
    and mothers and grandmothers
who have reason to grieve
    she keens; wildly, tenderly

She remembers
    her son's father
    dying of alcoholism

"I just got out of the psych ward.
I guess I went over the edge again.
I'm doing a lot of hunting
They say I don't drink so much
when I'm in the bush.
I'm saving money to come
and see my boys.
Please don't tell them.
I don't want them to get
disappointed."

She remembers
    the old man she met
    in old town
"You look just like my baby
    my baby   my baby
I didn't mean to hurt her
    I was drunk
    I was lonely
    I didn't know what I was doing.

Will you forgive me?"

She remembers
    mothers in the bars and children
    eating pop and chips in the lobby.
"That's me, the little fat kid in ragged shoes.
That little one, beside me, under my arm
that's my deceased sister.
And that's my brother.
He's doing 5 to 10 in Walla Walla.
My sister? She o.d'd in Van
She was seventeen.
Cops said she o.d'd
I know her pimp did it.
He knows I'll get him.
Sometime   somewhere

I'll get him."

She remembers
   her cousin's blood
    dried on the door of his truck
    dried on the floor of her auntie's truck
his blood
   melting the ground
   while three drug crazed relatives
   danced wildly in the snow.

She remembers
   taking 24 tranquilizers
   singing her death song
   thinking her sons would
   be better off without her
   hearing her Grandfather Josie
  saying
   "Get up, my girl.
   It's not your time to die."

So she lives
holding on to life; a new born baby,
feeding it, caring for it
tenaciously like a mother bear.
Like all the widows before her
she grieves in order to live,
to live a life so full of life
that grief will not kill it.

Her head throbs rhythmically
under and around the thickness
of the bandana.
She must remember the Thunderers
They are awakening
They are coming
seeking the ones like her

Were you There

for Joy Harjo

Were you there
on the White Sands?
Did you feel that primal wind
caressing the pores of your skin?
Did you smell the salt
of the old sea or
hear the silence roar
louder than the bombs
that blew on
Hiroshima or Nagasaki?

Were you there in Ottawa
when we rose as one
spontaneously
like a prayer for
all that we had been
and ever hoped to become?

Did you feel it then?
The whispered words of Beings
older than their laws or constitutions?

Were you there in the pine forest
in communion with those old trees
who keen for the people
laden with their burden
of grief and disrespect?

Were you there when the army
attacked the Kanesatake?
Did you feel the wind
shift
and blow the tear gas
back
on the Destroyers?

Were you there on the hill
when we called the Thunder?

It rained

and the land was green.

Return to Our Sacred Spaces

The Promise of Rain

I bathe in lavender
strong   earthen flowers
picked gently
in the early morning light.

My sweet body I offer you
buttermilk soft
yielding secrets too ancient
for words   man/woman
one like in the beginning
floating in our mutual sea.
Salt smell and sea sweat
coat our naked hope.

This vulnerable and venerable place
is where we dream
is where we find ourselves
more man   more woman
than before
more whole than in our separation.

The moon bathes us in her hope
that earth and sky will merge
have always merged   been one
but in our forgetting.

I bathe my body in lavender
earthen flower   waiting rain

For all the Settlers who Secretly Sing
for Sharon Butala

You have seen my ancestors
riding in buckskins
down the coulee.
You have watched
frightened. You who intrudes
awed, you who sees.

You have met the hawk
soaring as you sit
waiting for the land to speak
you, who have not heard her
since you fled across the seas.

You dream of drums
and hear voices singing
in the night sky
and wonder if the northern lights
are more than they appear.

You hold these questions
not daring to ask
the people who hold
themselves aloof from settler voices.
They think no one listens
and you understand
the stillness it requires
        and the faith
        and the faith
to hear the heart beat.

You dare not tell
her song rises in you
it rises and you sing
secretly   to the land
                to the land

She knows sister/brother
you belong
here, too.

Our Children

for GW

Our children will be
laser printed heartbeats
birthed in the waking
between words of other kinds.

Our children will travel
wrapped in leaves
electric pulsations
gathering speed
as we live and love and think our
dreams
spinning into strands of
sounds
woven in the heart.

Our children will grow
from earthen trees and stones
insinuating themselves
between the silent spaces
where no words have marched
warriors   wordsmithed in fires.

Our children will
take on this quest
this great adventure.

Her Face is Generic

Viewed from any angle, it shouts "Native."
A round face; brown and freckled
a hint of cheekbone beneath its plump surface.
Eyes, vaguely bear-like peek behind oval glasses,
a face so universally North American
Native child that any reservation north or south
of the line could claim it. Does she have long hair?
I suppose. Short, long, fluffy or straight,
no hairdo alters her pervasive "Indian-ness."
Supposing we add long straight black hair
to sway with her ambling walk;
testimony of her bear clan relations?
She combs her long hair
one braid behind her.
She wears a Navajo cut, blue jean skirt and
crisp cotton blouse. She smells of sage.

On reflection, I think
I'd better withdraw the long hair.
To add long hair might stereotype her image
so that only the hair's luster would linger
in the memory and the immutable pattern
of blood and bone spelled on her face
would fade like the face of First Woman
and the Thunderbeings who birthed her.

"Doesn't she look like Aunty Rose?"
Two Navajo sisters examine her face.

"Gee, I can't get over how much you look like my son!"
a Chippewa mother exclaims in awe.

"It makes me sad to look at you, " a Shuswap man tells her.
"You look like my late wife."

"Are you David McLeod's girl? Last time I saw your father..."

And they tell her stories about their relatives,
their adventures, their births, their deaths,
because her face mirrors them all
and they are not afraid of what is known.

Dancing With Rex

There's lightening in the sky
horses prancing in the wind
light and dark
playing tag around the big top.

There's dust devils flinging sand
on clouds travelling in groups
and Indians at a pow wow
promenading around the big top.

Aunty with her hand bag crosses
her hands demurely over her ample lap.
She sits tut tutting at all the
young clouds looking to score.

Me and Rex are brushing the dust
off our boots. His canine teeth
glint in the light of lightning
and his heart beats audibly in time to
the drums.

A nice sedate owl dance is starting,
under the big top.
Hey, Rex, says I, shall we dance?

Well now, girl,
says he, can you keep up with me?

Hey, Rex, says I, if I step on your feet
or grin too wide, it's just me
having a good time. Don't sweat
the small stuff.

Rex laughs a laugh, so big
you can count his teeth.

Hey, girl, that's all I want to know.

So we dance and Aunty watches
us closely. She doesn't like Rex
says he acts too smart,
shows off and never takes
things seriously.

We dance in time
        ta-dum
        ta-dum
        ta-dum
        ger-thunk
(that's Rex stepping on my feet)

Hey, don't sweat the small stuff.

Rex laughs so long and loud
that the old ladies shake their heads
and even the young men
        laugh nervously.

Woman's Stuff

for Mary Pitawanakwat, rest in peace.

Joanie's panty hose ripped
zzzip crunch
a whole leg from knee to ankle
ripped
ripped so bad   Joanie had no choice
but to phone in sick.

Mary, on hearing of her friend's plight,
drove up from Regina
to be with Joanie.

Mary knew panty hose was not the issue.

It was Joanie and her broken heart.

Woman's stuff
what was needed was:
        purple sweaters, silk scarves
        scented candles and
        Patsy Cline,

        a woman friend to while
        away the day with tears 'n talk;
        wrapped in an afghan
        soothed by chamomile tea.

Aretha sang blues back-up to
        Mary's commiserations
        and Joanie filled up.

When the day was done,
Joanie felt so much better
she rose from her sofa

went dancing
with cowboys at the Bar-K.

Mary popped into her car,

"Woman's stuff works every time," she said.

Devils and Angels

A naked lady air freshener hung from the rear view mirror
of the Mustang parked in our driveway; "Sleazy," I thought.

I walked the alley thinking about my roommate.
Michelle was partying
every night. I wondered
what would become of her.
Clouds and smog blackened the Vancouver sky
making ten a.m. seem like that dark hour before sunrise.
Why do all drunks come home then?

Michelle had come home,
I heard thumping, bumping, giggling and shushing.
"Don't wake my roommate," she said. The guy
had said nothing but then again,
a guy who hangs naked ladies
is the kind'a guy who's used to middle
of the night teepee creeps.

I got to the sky train. I flowed with the crowd,
"Michelle is not my responsibility," I thought
as I pushed down the aisle to an old man
talking to himself.
"Devils and angels, devils and angels."

The seat beside him was empty.
I sat down. I'm that kinda guy. What can I say?
The man was obviously "out there" but I was used to that.
My dad had been "out there" for as long as I knew him.
Good old Dad. I observed the old man.
He wore jeans, western shirt, and neckerchief,
a jean jacket and snow white Nikes.

"Devils and angels," he said to me.
His eyes clouded and watery,
his skin, leather smelling of wood smoke.

My father died when I was ten. He froze to death
on his way home from the bar.
I won't bore you with the details.
Mom was bummed big time. I don't remember
how I felt, but I remember the wood smoke
from the fire melting the ground for his grave.

The old man was still clutching my arm, "They all die," he said.
"What?" I couldn't help but ask, "Who dies?"
"All the devils and angels, son
They all die—some here, some over there." He gestured vaguely.

The air buzzed. Chills ran up and down my arms.
The old man nodded as if he knew
the sounds of the train, the people, and the noises of the city
died.
The old man spoke. "He did not choose life
but she will because you love her enough to leave her to it.
They've all the same —the loved and the unloved."

I looked into the old man's eyes
saw the snow falling on my father's grave.
That lanky ten year old falling
to his knees wailing, "Daddy, Daddy I love you."

He had never known. I had never told him.
My guts twisted. The old man on the sky train patted my arm.
He took my hands in his. They were warm and sandy.
"It's love that heals son," he said gently.
"Devils and angels, it don't matter who they are."
My face was wet. People were watching
the way people do when they understand
the need for privacy yet their need to know is stronger.

The old man said nothing more.
I squeezed his arm and rose to leave.
He extended his hand and I shook it.
I felt something in my hand,
but I was swept off the train.
When I freed myself from the wave of people
I opened my hand. It was a five dollar bill.
I gazed up at the old man on the train
and saw my dad, his crooked smile and that look
of glee every time he surprised me with the hand shake.

The sky train sped him away. He was still smiling
when it rounded the corner.

By Lund's Museum - 1954

This is where we visit
    where the grass is clean
    where the river runs,
northern families who
    smell of wood smoke and muskrat
    smoked hides and glass beads.

This is where the sounds of Cree
    and tea trickle in the wind
    where babies gurgle   dry and bundled
    while mama unwraps oatmeal
    cookies   sweet raison suns.

This is where I watch my brother
wolf down travelling bannock slathered in lard;
    (my skinny brother who all the ladies feed)
    the brother who will become a crusading
    filmmaker, politician, writer, and hockey dad.

This is where I watch my father
glide
    with the flow of protocol and custom
    handshakes and tobacco
    shared stories,   a nod.

This is where the summer sun
    soothes our souls, water
    lapping on sandy shores
where memory is taught with patience
    and poetry lurks in
    in the heart of one sturdy girl.

This is where we sit
by Lund's Museum
we northerners
who smell of wood smoke
and spruce gum
blueberries and birch.

We
will remember the clean grass
and the river
the smell of pine in the wind
and the clean knowing
that we belong
to this land
to this time.

Your Red Flesh

The strangers came in August
hot sun and tireless wind
told us the dusty farm truck
parked outside of town
cradled your warm red flesh
and I
delighted in the honey juice of you.

My face wet with your sensual caress
overflowed with pride
that I
this budding girl/woman
had set you free
my touch,   feather light
over your round firm body

I sliced you through
                    your red blood
flowed over dirty brown fingers
of brothers and sisters
who feasted on your flesh   and
spit your seed   to fertilize
another generation

of watermelon.

On Warm Air Like You

for GW

You snuggle
arm across my breasts
warm breath nuzzling my neck

The cat purrs at the foot of the bed.

I stretch and snuggle into you
kissing your round head
your ear, the valley between your lips.

This is our life.

The joy of this new sun
painting pink shadows
on the logs of our house;
eagles
soaring on warm air
rising from deep water.

"How do eagles keep warm
on days like this?" you muse.
We nestle in our blankets
and nest   skin to skin
Our easy breath mingles
with our laughter.

This is our life.

This celebration of ordinary moments
and the air
rising under our wings.

Ceremony for ending an affair of the heart

I give you back dear friend
Buffalo man   protector

You are free to go
      silently Buffalo
      softly as your hooves
      carry you back
      to prairie night wrapped in snow.

I give you back,

I release you your cradled arms
that held me.

I release you.

I release you your Buffalo voice
that taught me to fly.

I release you.

I release you your man heart whose
love was never spoken.

I release you.

I release you your pain on leaving
me   a woman now.

I release you.

I give you back dear friend
Buffalo man   protector.